Dear Educators, Parents, and Caregivers,

Welcome to Penguin Core Concepts! The Core Concepts program exposes children to a diverse range of literary and informational texts, which will help them develop important literacy and cognitive skills necessary to meet many of the Common Core State Standards (CCSS).

The Penguin Core Concepts program includes twenty concepts (shown on the inside front cover of this book), which cover major themes that are taught in the early grades. Each book in the program is assigned one or two core concepts, which tie into the content of that particular book.

The Firefighter covers the concepts Community Workers & Helpers and Problem Solving. The social studies concept Community Workers & Helpers can be used as a way to expose students to a diverse range of literary and informational texts, as recommended in the CCSS for English Language Arts & Literacy. The concept Problem Solving can help students develop important cognitive skills necessary to meet many of the CCSS, such as how to engage creativity and imagination to make predictions. After you've read the book, here are some questions/ideas to get your discussions started:

- Why are firefighters important members of the community?

- Discuss what to do, and the right precautions to take, if there is a fire at home or at school.

- This story is fiction, yet it is filled with facts. Make a list of the equipment the firefighter used.

Above all, the books in the Penguin Core Concepts program have engaging stories with fantastic illustrations and/or photographs, and are a perfect way to instill the love of reading in a child!

Bonnie Bader, EdM
Editor in Chief, Penguin Core Concepts

the Firefighter

For all my firefighter friends and family—particularly my husband, Matt, and my brother, James—thanks for everything you do!—JG

To Studio Armad'illo—AP

GROSSET & DUNLAP
Penguin Young Readers Group
An Imprint of Penguin Random House LLC

Penguin supports copyright. Copyright fuels creativity, encourages diverse voices, promotes free speech, and creates a vibrant culture. Thank you for buying an authorized edition of this book and for complying with copyright laws by not reproducing, scanning, or distributing any part of it in any form without permission. You are supporting writers and allowing Penguin to continue to publish books for every reader.

Text copyright © 2015 by Jenny Goebel. Illustrations copyright © 2015 by Penguin Random House LLC. All rights reserved. Published by Grosset & Dunlap, an imprint of Penguin Random House LLC, 345 Hudson Street, New York, New York 10014. GROSSET & DUNLAP is a trademark of Penguin Random House LLC. Manufactured in China.

Library of Congress Cataloging-in-Publication Data is available.

ISBN 978-0-448-48101-2 (pbk)   10 9 8 7 6 5 4 3 2 1
ISBN 978-0-448-48102-9 (hc)   10 9 8 7 6 5 4 3 2 1

by Jenny Goebel
illustrated by Alessandra Psacharopulo

Grosset & Dunlap
An Imprint of Penguin Random House

The firefighter sleeps, snug and sound in his bed.

Then *BRR-RING* go the bells, and up pops his head.

He leaps to his feet, and he slides down the pole.

He pulls on his boots, and he's ready to roll.

We-OOO goes the siren, and bright red lights flash.
The station doors fly open. They're off in a dash!

The fire truck roars as it zips down the street.
The firefighter bumps and sways in his seat.

The fire captain shouts, "Pull over right here!"
The truck squeals to a stop. The crew puts on their gear.

They yank helmets on heads, masks over noses,
then go to the hydrant and drag out the hoses.

A firefighter says as he bandages a scrape,
"Your family is lucky. You were able to escape."
The little boy says, "We rushed out in a hurry.
Are the puppies all safe?" The family starts to worry.

The Dalmatians are counted again and again.
Nine black-and-white pups, but where's number ten?

The firefighter says, "Don't worry, we'll help."
Then, from inside the house, they hear a faint yelp.

The firefighter is scared. It's tough to be brave. But still he must go—there's a puppy to save!

He swings an ax hard, and he chops through the door.
He pushes inside and drops down on all fours.

The smoke is thick as he crawls down the hall.
He breathes through his mask and stays close to the wall.

Where are you? he thinks as he searches the dark.
The firefighter stops. He hears another bark!

"I've got you," he says, and he hugs the pup tight.
Then reports to his crew, "It's okay. She's all right!"

The family's relieved. Their smiles are wide as the firefighter races the puppy outside.

The crew keeps on fighting. They work long and hard.

The fire's extinguished. All ten puppies are fine.

The firefighter is happy. He leaves behind nine . . .

Back at the station, the crew stows their gear.

Then they come together and give a big cheer.

The firefighter grins and scoops his pal up.

"Welcome home," he says, "little firehouse pup!"

Worn out and tired, he climbs back into bed.
He hears a grateful *woof,* and up pops his head.

The firefighter shushes, "Not another peep!"

Then he and the pup, snug and sound, go to sleep.